# LITTLE LEMUR LAUGHING

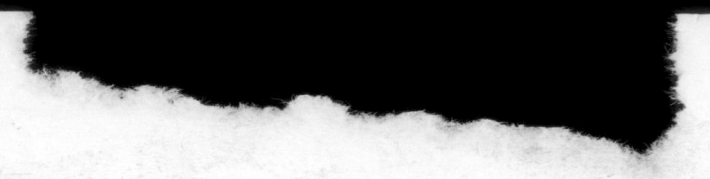

Bloomsbury Education
An imprint of Bloomsbury Publishing Plc

50 Bedford Square
London
WC1B 3DP
UK

1385 Broadway
New York
NY 10018
USA

www.bloomsbury.com

BLOOMSBURY and the Diana logo are trademarks of Bloomsbury Publishing Plc

First published in 2017 by Bloomsbury Education

ISBN

PB:      978-1-4729-3004-0
ePub:    978-1-4729-3006-4
ePDF:    978-1-4729-3007-1

2  4  6  8  10  9  7  5  3  1

Printed and bound in CPI Group (UK) Ltd, Croydon CR0 4YY

MIX
Paper from
responsible sources
FSC® C020471

To find out more about our authors and books visit www.bloomsbury.com. Here you will find extracts,
author interviews, details of forthcoming events and the option to sign up for our newsletters.

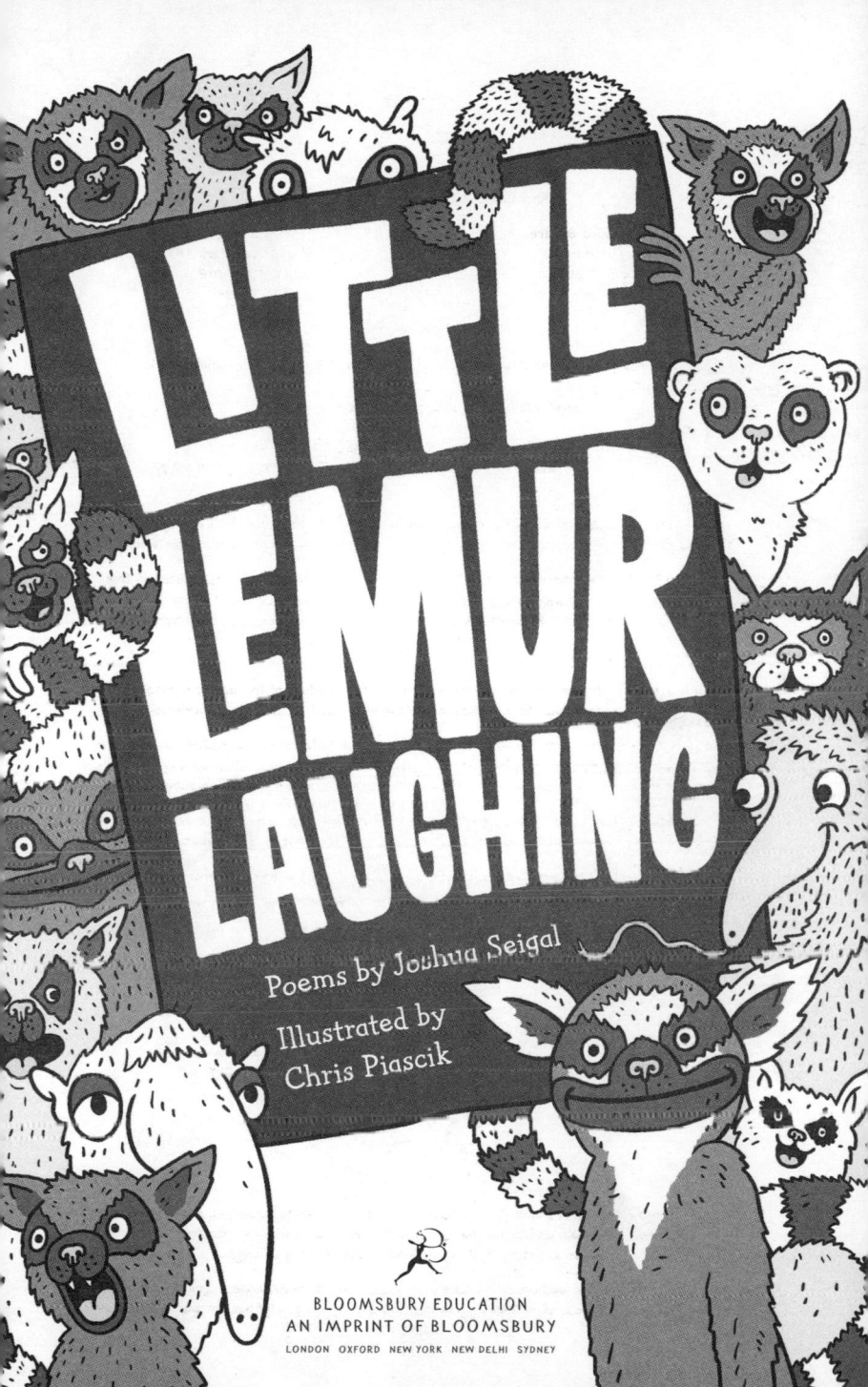

# LITTLE LEMUR LAUGHING

Poems by Joshua Seigal

Illustrated by
Chris Piascik

BLOOMSBURY EDUCATION
AN IMPRINT OF BLOOMSBURY

LONDON   OXFORD   NEW YORK   NEW DELHI   SYDNEY

# Contents

## What's In A Poem?

A busy buzzy
bumblebee,
a happy hopping
wallaby,
a cheeky chatty
chimpanzee –
that's what's in a poem.

A scrumptious slice
of birthday cake,
an ice cream with
a chocolate flake,
a tray of biscuits
freshly baked –
that's what's in a poem.

A zooming car,
a chuffing train,
an empty house,
a winding lane,
a holiday
in southern Spain –
that's what's in a poem.

A dragon's sneeze,
a dinosaur,
a wizard's spell,
a monster's claw.
All these things
and many more –
that's what's in a poem.

## Lemurs

lively lemur leaping
in the branches of a tree

lazy lemur lying
down and sleeping happily

lucky lemur licking
at a luscious little leaf

loving lemur latching
to her mother underneath

little lemur laughing
having lots of fun today

lonely lemur longing
for a friend to come and play.

## What Am I Like?

I'm like a cheeky monkey
when I'm standing on my head

I'm like a stubborn mule
because I will not go to bed

I'm like a messy pig
because my room is like a sty

I'm like a grumpy elephant
because I sometimes cry

I'm like a dashing cheetah
when I'm darting home from school

I'm like a graceful dolphin
when I'm swimming in the pool

I'm like a lazy lion
when I'm lying in the sun

and being like an animal
is such a lot of fun!

## Daddy Long Legs

*Daddy Long Legs*
*Daddy Long Legs*

crawling up
the kitchen wall

*Daddy Long Legs*
*Daddy Long Legs*

is he scary?
not at all!

*Daddy Long Legs*
*Daddy Long Legs*

he's not yucky
he's not mean

*Daddy Long Legs*
*Daddy Long Legs*

why does he
make Mummy scream?

## Which Are Better?

Which are better,
cats or dogs?
Dogs go for walks
and cats sleep like logs.
Cats chase mice
and dogs wag their tails,
but I don't care –
*I prefer snails.*

Which are better,
birds or bees?
Bees make honey
and birds live in trees.
Birds have nice feathers,
especially the males,
but I don't care –
*I prefer snails.*

Which are better,
goldfish or gerbils?
Goldfish swim around
in their fishbowl.
Gerbils can scratch you
with their nails,
but I don't care –
*I prefer snails.*

Which are better,
dolphins or whales?
Whales are big
and dolphins are graceful.
Whales or dolphins?
Dolphins or whales?
For the last time, who cares?
*I prefer snails!*

I AM A LITTLE FRUIT BAT AND I'M BATTY ABOUT FRUIT. FOR BROCCOLI AND CELERY I DO NOT GIVE A HOOT. I'M NOT AN OWL, A CENTIPEDE, AN OTTER OR A NEWT, FOR I'M A LITTLE FRUIT BAT AND I'M BATTY ABOUT FRUIT

# I

## AM A
### LITTLE BAT'S FRUIT
### AND I'M FRUITY ABOUT BATS.
# I'M NOT A SWEDE, A PEA,
### A SPROUT OR ANYTHING LIKE THAT.
### I DO NOT CARE FOR OSTRICHES
## OR ANTELOPES OR CATS,
## FOR I'M A LITTLE
### BAT'S FRUIT AND
#### I'M FRUITY ABOUT
## BATS.

## Snake

Snake

Slimy snake

Slithery slimy snake

Soft slithery slimy snake

Snappy soft slithery slimy snake

Scary snappy soft slithery slimy snake

Ssssssssssssssssssssssssssssssssssssssss!

## Kennel Kennings

Doorbell-barker

    Hand-licker

Bed-climber

    Noisy-yapper

Cautious-greeter

    Fussy-eater

Squirrel-chaser

    Deep-sleeper

River-wallower

    Little-follower

Lazy-log –

    It's my dog.

## My Dog Eats Spaghetti!

My dog eats spaghetti!
He slurps it with bliss.
My dog eats spaghetti!
It sounds just like this:

Sthfhthflthflthfhtlfhtlfhtlfhtlfhtlhtldefertldfpp

My dog eats spaghetti!
He thinks it's a treat,
and this is the sound
that he makes when he eats:

Sthfhthflthflthfhtlfhtlfhtlfhtlfhtlhtldefertldfpp

My dog eats spaghetti!
He sure needs a muzzle,
for this is the sound
that he makes when he guzzles:

Sthfhthflthflthfhtlfhtlfhtlfhtlfhtlhtldefertldfpp

My dog eats spaghetti!
He slurps it with bliss.
My dog eats spaghetti!
It sounds just like this:

Sthfhthflthflthfhtlfhtlfhtlfhtlfhtlhtldefertldfpp

## Doggy

*Yap Yap Yap!*
Doggy on my lap.

*Bark Bark Bark!*
Doggy in the park.

*Ruff Ruff Ruff!*
Doggy had enough.

*Can't hear a peep –*
Doggy fast asleep.

LllllllllllllllllllllllllllLllama!

I'm thinking of an animal
who has the longest name,
and saying it out loud
can be a quite amusing game,
so say it with me now
and there will be no need for drama –

it's a lllllllllllllllllllllllllllllama!

I'm thinking of an animal
whose fur is soft and fluffy.
If it doesn't get a haircut
then it gets all long and scruffy,
so come and shear its coat
and make some luxury pyjamas –

it's a lllllllllllllllllllllllllllllama!

I'm thinking of an animal
that some might say is cute,
but if you are not careful
it can be a beastly brute.
It likes to spit ferociously
so wear a suit of armour –

it's a lllllllllllllllllllllllllllllllama!

I'm thinking of an animal
whose name is fun to rhyme,
so say it loud and proud
and you will have a super time.
It sounds a bit like 'farmer';
it's not President Obama –

it's a lllllllllllllllllllllllllllllllama!

## Seagulls

seagulls, seagulls
swirling, swooping

seagulls, seagulls
loop-the-looping

seagulls, seagulls
screeching, squalling

seagulls, seagulls
caterwauling

seagulls, seagulls
flapping, flocking

seagulls, seagulls
madly mocking

seagulls, seagulls
doing dips

seagulls, seagulls
stealing chips!

## The Sea

The sea! The sea!
I'm feeling bold
*I dip my toe in...*
    **IT'S TOO COLD!**

The sea! The sea!
Come with me, Mum!
*I dip my toe in...*
    **FOOT'S GONE NUMB!**

The sea! The sea!
How blue! How nice!
*I dip my toe in...*
    **FEELS LIKE ICE!**

The sea! The sea!
Looks calm and pleasing
*Dip my toe in...*
    **OUCH! IT'S FREEZING!**

## Sand

There's sand in my ears
and sand in my hair.
There's sand in my t-shirt
that shouldn't be there.

There's sand in my ice cream
and sand in my coat.
There's sand up my nostrils
and sand in my throat.

There's sand in my towel
and under my nails.
There's sand in my shoes
leaving long sandy trails.

There's sand lodged in places
I cannot quite reach.
There's more sand on me
than there is on the beach!

## Man On The Beach

Where is he going?
Where has he been?
Where does he come from?
What has he seen?
Why is he limping?
Is he in pain?
Why is he walking
alone in the rain?

Does he feel jolly?
Does he feel sad?
Does he have children?
Is he a dad?
Are his hands freezing?
Is his coat warm?
Why is he walking
alone in the storm?

## Remembering

As the thunder rolls
I remember better times:

friends building castles
with my warm golden sand;

kids catching crabs
in my cool salty rock pools;

families lounging on me,
seagulls swooping overhead;

waves lapping lightly,
licking at my shore.

Now the cold rain tumbles
and the angry wind howls,

and I lie empty,
remembering.

I'M VERY TALL.
MY HEAD IS HIGH.
MY LIPS REACH OUT
TO KISS THE SKY.
MY EARS CAN HEAR FOR
MILES AROUND.

I STAND ONE-LEGGED ON THE GROUND.

## Body Poem

I **hear** with my **ears**
and I **tap** with my **toes**.

My **bottom** it **sits**
and my **arm** it **throws**.

My mouth it **SHOUTS**
and as for my **nose** –

it **sniffs** and it **snorts**
and it **twitches** and **blows**!

My **legs** they **run** –
just watch them go –

but let me say something
I want you to know:

some bits do **a lot**
but the best does **nothing** –

It's this thing right here,
**my belly button!**

My Hand

IT HOLDS, IT FOLDS. IT CARES, IT SHARES,

IT FLICKS, IT PLAYS WITH STICKS. IT SCOLDS, MY CLOTHES IT

IT CLICKS, IT WAVES. IT MISBEHAVES.

IT CLAPS, IT WAVES,

IT TICKLES BEARS!!

## We're Having A Party!

We're having a party!
What can you **see?**
Bouncing balloons
and sparkly ribbons.

We're having a party!
What can you **hear?**
Toe-tapping tunes
and chuckling children.

We're having a party!
What can you **smell?**
The flickering flame
of birthday candles.

We're having a party!
What can you **taste?**
Sandwiches, cake
and plenty of sweets.

We're having a party!
What can you **feel?**
The love and the hugs
from all of your friends.

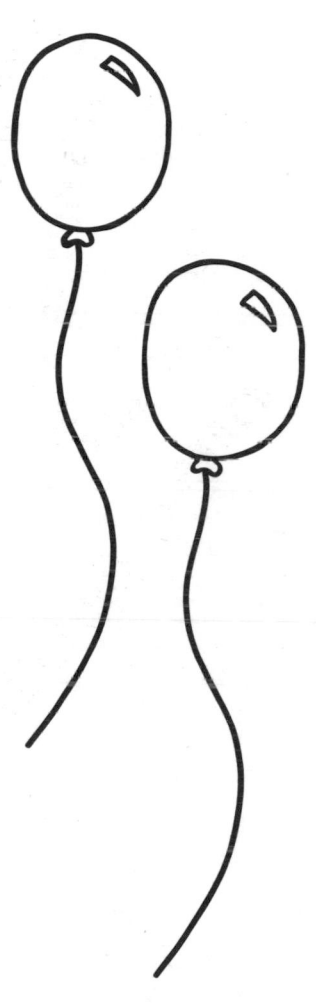

## When I Dance

When I dance
I flap my arms!

When I dance
I rub my tum!

When I dance
I pound my chest!

When I dance
I shake my bum!

When I dance
I jump up high!

When I dance
I touch the ground!

When I dance
I nod my head!

When I dance
I twirl around!

## Friends

Loud friends, shy friends,
help-me-when-I-cry friends,
friends who like to push me on the swings.
Silly friends, mad friends,
happy friends and sad friends,
friends who bring me lots of lovely things.

Jumping friends, clapping friends,
singing, rhyming, rapping friends,
friends who like to chase me in the park.
Naughty friends, caring friends,
generous and sharing friends,
friends who tell me stories after dark.

Big friends, small friends,
tiny friends and tall friends,
Alice, Evie, Ahmed, Raj and Sam.
Old friends, new friends,
stick-to-me-like-glue friends,
friends who like me just the way I am.

## Come Yab With Me!

I'm all alone
I can see that you are too
I have a great idea
I know what we should do
Come **yab** with me
Let's **yab** together
Let's **yab** 'til our hearts
Are content
Let's **yab** all day
I can honestly say
It'll be a day's **yab**bing
Well spent
And then we might
**Yab** all night
And all of tomorrow too
I can promise sincerely
That I would love dearly
To spend my life **yab**bing
With you
With you
To spend my life **yab**bing
With you

(What is **yab**bing?
Can't you see –
It can be whatever
*You* want it to be!)

## Conkers

I found this one
outside my house.

I picked this one up
when I went to the park.

These ones I gathered
on the field at school

and this one I got
from my best friend Tom.

I plucked this one
straight off the branch.

I nicked this one
from my sister's room.

These ones I won
in a playground game

and this one I found
in my secret place.

## My Coat

My coat is as soft
as a fleecy young lamb.

My coat protects me,
like a tortoise's shell.

My coat is yellow,
like a smiling sun.

My coat is my armour
against the wind.

My coat keeps winter out,
and summer in.

## Snow School Today!

There's snow school
There's snow school
There's snow school today!

There's snow school
There's snow school
There's snow school today!

We'll run and play
And shout *hooray* –
The school has closed;
Let's get our sleigh!

There's no school
There's no school
There's no school today!

## Fireworks

A dash of red
A splash of blue
A splodge of green
and a twinkle of gold.

A streak of white
A stripe of pink
A smear of yellow
and a sparkle of silver.

Somewhere, a happy child
is flicking paint
across the sky.

DEAR SPRING,
I'M WRITING YOU
THIS LETTER,
TO ASK WHETHER
YOU'D CONSIDER,
NOT COMING
THIS YEAR.
THIS QUESTION
MAY COME AS QUITE
A SURPRISE, FOR I KNOW
MOST PEOPLE ARE GLAD
WHEN YOU ARRIVE,
BUT PLEASE STOP AND THINK ABOUT ME!
I CRAVE THE COLD AND I NEED THE ICE.
SO PLEASE, SPRING –
WHAT DO YOU SAY?
I CAN ALREADY FEEL
MYSELF FADING AWAY.

YOURS, MR. SNOWMAN

## The Worst Thing About Summer

The... ACHOO!
worst... ACHOO!
thing... ACHOO!
about... ACHOO!
summer... ACHOO!
is... ACHOOOOOOOOOOOOOOOOOOOOOOOOOOOOOOOOOOOOOOOOOOOOOOOOOOOOOOOOOOOOOOOOOOO!!!

hay fever.

Apple

SEE THE
APPLE
CHOOSE THE APPLE
BUY THE APPLE-
YUM!

WASH THE
APPLE
CUT THE APPLE...
WILL YOU DO IT
MUM?

Liquorice

LIQUORICE, LIQUORICE, WIRY AND WICKERISH, GIVE ME A PIECE AND I'LL HAVE IT FOR TEA.

LIQUORICE, LIQUORICE, NO NEED TO BICKER. THERE'S ONE PIECE FOR YOU

AND THERE'S ONE PIECE FOR ME!

## Don't Go To The Cake Shop!

Legs of frog

     Tail of rat

Paws of dog

     Whiskers of cat

Slime of slug

     Shell of snail

Pin of porcupine

     Blubber of whale

Beaver's tongue

     Lion's mane

Bark from a tree

     Goo from the drain

Scales of snake

and beak of puffin –

That's what goes into

a blueberry muffin.

# Johnny And The **MANGO!**

Johnny wouldn't eat his tea:
his mum had given him celery,
which Johnny didn't want, you see
all Johnny liked was **MANGO!**

Johnny wouldn't eat his lunch:
his mum had given him crisps to munch,
but Johnny wanted a bowl of punch
made with lots and lots of **MANGO!**

Johnny wouldn't eat his sandwich:
It had cheese and it had ham
with peanut butter and strawberry jam,
but Johnny wanted **MANGO!**

Now Jonny liked his mango.
It was his favourite fruit.
He liked it more than chocolate,
and more than his pet newt.
He really loved his mango
and you might just start to laugh
when I tell you where he liked to eat it –
he ate it in the *bath!*

Johnny's mum said "have a shower",
but Johnny gave an angry glower.
He wanted a bath at this wee hour
so he could eat his **MANGO!**

So Johnny got himself undressed,
he took off his socks, took off his vest,
and went to the kitchen and made a mess
looking for some **MANGO!**

Johnny went into the larder,
he reached for the shelf – *Harder! Harder!*
He knew just what he was after,
he was trying to find a **MANGO!**

*And then...*

Johnny found a mango,
and hid it from his mum.
He went into the bathroom
so he could have some fun.
He ran himself a nice hot bath,
now he was really free,
and he got into the water
and had **MANGO** for his tea!

# Paper Soup

*Paper soup*
*Paper soup*
Rip the pieces up

*Paper soup*
*Paper soup*
Put them in a cup

*Paper soup*
*Paper soup*
Stir it round and round

*Paper soup*
*Paper soup*
Listen to the sound

*Paper soup*
*Paper soup*
Have a little taste

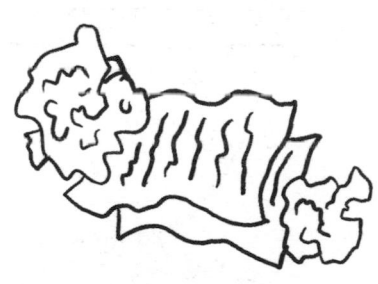

*Paper soup*
*Paper soup*
Pull a funny face!

## Turvy & Topsy

A boy was walking
down the street
with pointy shoes
upon his... head.

A girl who passed
the other way
said "what a bright
and sunny... hat."

The boy replied,
"it hurts my head!
I'd rather be
asleep in... a barn".

The girl look shocked,
then gave a bawl:
"this poem makes
no sense at... MOO!"

## The Queen Of Halloween

My skin is pale
My fangs are mean
My nose is long
My tongue is green
My hair is red
I look obscene
I am the Queen
Of Halloween!

My eyes are wide
My sight is keen
My breath's not nice
My clothes aren't clean
I'll make you **SHOUT!**
I'll make you **SCREAM!**
I am the Queen
Of Halloween!

## Monsters

Big ones
Small ones
Very very tall ones
This one is a cool one!

**Roar! ROAR! ROAR!!**

Jolly one
Proud one
Fluffy-like-a-cloud one
This one is a loud one!

# Roar! ROAR! ROAR!!

Wet one
Dry one
Flying-in-the-sky-one
Tiny little shy one!

**Roar! ROAR! ROAR!!**

Green one
Red one
Standing-on-its-head one
Sleeping-in-your-bed one!

**Snore! SNORE! SNORE!!**

I'm a Brontosaurus
*Stomp! Stomp! Stomp!*

I take my baths in a
*Swamp! Swamp! Swamp!*

I munch on leaves with a
*Chomp! Chomp! Chomp!*

I'm a Brontosaurus
*Stomp! Stomp! Stomp!*

## Stickers

I went to fetch the register.
I got my spellings right.
I put my hand up nicely
and I didn't fuss or fight.

I finished all my sandwiches.
I drank up all my drink.
I washed the art equipment
that was lying in the sink.

I wrote the longest story
and I did the hardest sum.
I didn't laugh in circle time
or wail for my mum.

I didn't lose my jumper
and I didn't wet my knickers,
and that is why my teacher
gave me all these lovely STICKERS!

## Colours

**Green** is the colour
of a hopping frog.

**Brown** is the colour
of a yapping dog.

**Black** is the colour
of the night-time sky.

**Red** is the colour
of a cherry pie.

**Blue** is the colour
of my mummy's car.

Look at all the **colours**
of the sweets in the jar!

## Colouring In

I'm colouring in.
I'm colouring in.
Some people draw
or build wonderful things.
Some go outside
and they play on the swings,
but I'm just
colouring in.

I sit in a corner,
I'm doing just fine
with my colouring pens,
keeping tight to the lines.
I stick out my tongue
and I hum and I sing,
while I'm
colouring in.

In fact I'm the best
colour-inner in class.
I fail most tests
but this one I pass.
I lose at most games
but at this one I win –
yes I love
colouring in.

## Uncle

Understands difficult words

Never tells me off or shouts

Can remember lots of jokes, and

Laughs when he tells them

Everyone deserves an uncle like mine

## Chat

I have a mum who likes to chat.
She chats to the dog
and she chats to the cat.
She chats about this
and she chats about that.
She chats on the telephone –

**CHAT! CHAT! CHAT!**

She chats in the kitchen.
She chats in the street.
She chats to the neighbours
and people she meets.
She chats about this
and she chats about that.
She chats on the internet –

**CHAT! CHAT! CHAT!**

She chats in the morning.
She chats in the night.
She chats when it's dark
and she chats when it's light.
She chats about this
and she chats about that.
She chats in the supermarket –

**CHAT! CHAT! CHAT!**

I have a mum who likes to chat.
She chats to my aunt
and to Great Uncle Pat.
She chats about this
and she chats about that.
All she ever does is

**CHAT! CHAT! CHAT!**

# Performing Monkey

I'm not a performing monkey
I don't live in the zoo
I'm not a performing monkey
I don't go OO! OO! OO!

I'm not a performing monkey
I don't swing in a tree
I'm not a performing monkey
I don't go OO-EE-EEE!

I'm not a performing monkey
I'm not a go-rill-a
I'm not a performing monkey
I don't go OO-AH-AH!

I'm not a performing monkey
I don't live in the zoo
But as a special treat
I'll do this poem
Just for you!

Butterfly

BUTTERFLY )( FLUTTERS
BY, TUMBLING TUMBLING
THROUGH THE SKY, LANDING
SOFTLY ON MY NOSE
FLICK IT OFF
—AWAY IT GOES...

## My Pet Nothing

I have a pet nothing.
Its name is

It's very easy to look after:
it doesn't eat anything

or take up any space;
it doesn't leave hair all over the couch,

or go to the toilet on the carpet;
it never gets lost, or muddy,

and it doesn't scratch at the door.
My friends prefer cats and dogs –

they think my pet nothing
is boring,

but my pet nothing
is my best friend in the world.

My last pet died, but I know
my pet nothing

never will.

## Rainbow

Everywhere I go
I carry a rainbow.
They say that at the end
of a rainbow
lies a pot of gold.
With this rainbow
under my arm
the whole world
is my treasure.

## Let's Play...

*[deep breath]*

... goodies and baddies
and mummies and daddies
and doctors and nurses
and writers of verses
and cops and then robbers
and robbers and cops
and let's skip and let's jump
and let's run and let's hop
and let's go wild
and let's play dead
and let's crack eggs
and let's bake bread
and let's play goats
and let's play sheep
and let's go upstairs
and go off to sleep.

# When Granny Tucks Me In

The sea is still,
the wind is warm,
there is no rain,
there is no storm,
there is no need
to be forlorn
when Granny tucks me in.

The grass is green,
the clouds are white,
the trees are lush,
the sky is bright,
there's no such thing
as darkest night
when Granny tucks me in.

There is no fog,
there is no gloom,
the bunnies hop,
the flowers bloom,
the sun starts shining
in my room
when Granny tucks me in.

The heavens sing
with graceful bliss.
There's just one thing
I wouldn't miss –
that yucky, gooey, sticky kiss
when Granny tucks me in!

## Get Writing!

Hello! Joshua here. I had a lot of fun writing the poems in this book, and I hope you have had great fun reading them, whispering them and perhaps even SCREAMING them out loud! There are lots of different types of poems in this book, and you and your friends might like to have a go at writing some poems yourselves. Here are some ideas to help get you started.

## Amazing Animal Alliteration

My poem 'Lemurs' uses *alliteration*. This means that lots of the lines have words which all start with the same letter, for example 'lively lemur leaping' and 'little lemur laughing'. To write this type of poem, first pick an animal. After you've chosen your *animal*, think of a word to *describe* it, and then think of an *action* that your animal is doing. Try to make all these words start with the same letter, for example:

*pretty penguin paddling*
*tiny tiger trembling*
*cute cat cuddling.*

Once you've got your list of amazing alliterative animals, you can complete the sentences to create the lines for your poem:

*pretty penguin paddling in a pool*
*tiny tiger trembling in its cage*
*cute cat cuddling on the sofa...*

## Animal Steps

In my poem 'Snake', I added a word on each line, so the lines get longer and longer. To write this type of poem, write the name of an animal as your first line. Then, on the next line, repeat the name of the animal, but this time add another word before it. Then, on the next line, add another word, and keep repeating this for as long as you like! Remember to make the words interesting and imaginative. Here is another example of mine to help you get started:

*Monkey*
*Cheeky monkey*
*Swooping cheeky monkey*
*Laughing swooping cheeky monkey...*

## Question Poems

My poem 'Man on the Beach' is made up of
questions. You can do something similar; just
pick an object and write questions about it.
I can see a tree out of my window. Here are
some questions I might ask the tree:

*When were you born?*
*What is the most interesting thing you've seen?*
*What makes you angry?*

If you are feeling really adventurous, you
could develop the poem by writing answers to
the questions:

*When were you born?*
*I was born when the seed cracked to reveal a*
*universe...*

## The Five Senses

Your five senses are your most crucial poetic tools. My poem 'We're Having a Party' uses each of my five senses. You can do something similar. Imagine you are somewhere fun and exciting, like a swimming pool on a summer's day. Write a poem with five verses, and in each verse use one of your five senses. The first two verses might go like this:

*I can **see** people*
*diving into the*
*cool blue water.*

*I can **hear** the crashing*
*and screaming of*
*excited children...*

## Colours

My poem 'Colours' is very easy to imitate.
Start by picking a colour, and then describe
something that has that colour. So you might
get lines like this:

*Red is the colour of a wailing fire engine*
*Blue is the colour of the swirling ocean*
*Pink is the colour of my baby brother's cheeks*

If you want to make this really interesting,
do it with your friends and have a competition
to see who can come up with the strangest,
most imaginative ideas. Here is my strangest
idea – see if you can beat it:

*Orange is the colour of the fire in a baby*
*dragon's heart...*

## Acknowledgements

'Man on the Beach' originally appeared in *Poems About the Seaside*, Brian Moses (ed.), Wayland (2015).

'Performing Monkey' originally appeared in *Off By Heart: Poems for Children to Learn and Remember*, Roger Stevens (ed.), Bloomsbury (2013).